THROUGH MY EYES

BY TAMMY WILSON

Illustration by Jill Dubbeldee Kuhn

ISBN 13: 978-1-59298-698-9
Library of Congress Catalog Number: 2015920381
Printed in the United States of America .
First Printing: 2016
20 19 18 17 16   5 4 3 2 1
Book design and typesetting by Dan Pitts
Illustrated by Jill Dubbeldee Kuhn © copyright 2016

BEAVER'S POND
PRESS

Beaver's Pond Press
7108 Ohms Lane
Edina, MN 55439–2129
(952) 829-8818
www.BeaversPondPress.com

To order, visit www.BeaversPondBooks.com
or call (800)-901-3480. Reseller discounts available.

I dedicate this book to my three amazing children—
Nick, Mike, and Ashley. I will always believe in you.
-Tammy

I dedicate this artwork to my three kind children—
Sienna, Ivy, and Turner (and snow angels everywhere).
-Jill

ACKNOWLEDGMENTS:

I would like to acknowledge Rahma Youssouf, Aswan Mohamed, Zakia Aden, Abdimalik Abdulahi, Roda Nur, and Abduhakim Hassan. It has been an honor to be in your presence as you so bravely shared your remarkable stories with me. I will never forget special moments like when you danced freely to your music or when you spoke from your heart about what matters to you. Thank you for your trust.

Thank you Mubashir Abib, Neim Salah, Najah Shire, Suad Ali, and Asha Omar for your willingness to pose for pictures. I think you will enjoy seeing how they unfolded into illustrations in the book. You did a great job!

I would like to give a special thanks to Bishar Hassan, Mohamed Ukash, and Abdirizak Abdi, as you have helped me gain a better understanding of your culture and religious beliefs. Nimo Warfa and Ikram Ibrahim, you are strong, beautiful, and courageous. Thank you for sharing your incredible journey with me. I can't wait to see what your future holds. It has been a privilege to know all of you.

CONTENTS

PREFACE:

I am an elementary principal at a school with a highly diverse population. When there was an influx of Somali students, teachers expressed a desire to learn more about the Somali culture in order to provide all their students with opportunities for success. Although caring and compassionate, many teachers didn't realize the intelligence and potential of the Somali children due to a language barrier. I saw a need to educate others about the richness of what Somali students have to offer and the fact that no matter where we were born, we are more alike than different.

Another goal was to add literature and reading materials for my Somali students so they would see themselves reflected in their school. When I couldn't find children's stories about Somali experiences, I decided to write such a book. The purpose was to give Somali students a voice and to educate others about their culture. There are lessons about compassion, tolerance, and acceptance.

Although some of the events described and some of the characters in this book may be based on actual events and real people, Zamzam is a fictional character created by the author; Zamzam's diary and scenes are also works of fiction. Character attributes were created based on universal themes that are global and that any human being may possess.

INTRODUCTION

HISTORY

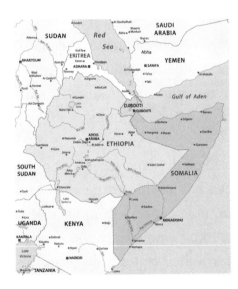

Somalia was forever changed when a civil war broke out in 1991. Parts of this beautifully landscaped country with palm trees, beaches, and oceans are now in ruins. The dictator Mohamed Siad Barre, who ruled the Somali Democratic Republic since 1969, was forced to flee when rival clan militias captured the capital of Mogadishu. Somalia has been without a stable central government since the ruler was ousted in 1991. Different clans have been fighting over land and resources ever since. The fighting flared with little warning; kidnapping, murder, and other threats to foreigners still occur unpredictably in many regions.

Since 1991, an estimated 350,000 to 1,000,000 Somalis have died because of the conflict. Over 400,000 Somalis have died from starvation.

While the civil war has affected many areas of Somalia, other areas are flourishing. For example, Mogadishu, the capital of Somalia, earned its nickname the White Pearl because of its history as a beach resort for Italians and other Europeans, with luxury hotels on beautiful beaches. In some cases, businesses continue to thrive, the education system remains strong, and Somalis successfully contribute to their community.

Through My Eyes is based on the experiences of Somali people who have been hardest hit by the aftermath of the civil war and continued attacks from terrorists. Refugees remain a close-knit community and continue to embody the values of their culture, like peacefulness and generosity.

Somalis are Muslims and faithfully practice Islam. Islam is both a religion and a complete way of life following the tenets of peace, mercy, and forgiveness.

ISLAM

Islam is one of the largest religions in the world. There are an estimated 1.2 billion Muslims worldwide. No more than 20 percent of Muslims live in the Arabic-speaking world. There are an estimated seven million Muslims in America.

The Muslim community in America is made up of a wide variety of ethnic backgrounds and national origins. There are almost two thousand mosques, Islamic schools, and Islamic centers in America.

Muslims are active in all walks of life, and Islam is one of the fastest-growing religions in this country and around the world.

Muslims are monotheistic: they believe in one unique God, the creator of the universe; it is believed that God spoke through a chain of prophets beginning with Adam and included Noah, Abraham, Ishmael, Isaac, Jacob, Joseph, Job, Moses, David, Solomon, and Jesus. God's eternal message was then reaffirmed and finalized by the Prophet Muhammad (peace be on them all).

One becomes a Muslim by saying, "There is no deity but God, and Muhammad is the messenger of God." By this declaration, the person announces faith in all God's messengers.

THE PILLARS OF ISLAM

There are Five Pillars of Islam. The first Pillar is the **Declaration of Faith**: there is no deity but God, and Muhammad is the messenger of God.

The second Pillar is **Prayer**. Muslims perform five obligatory prayers each day. Islamic prayers are a direct link between the worshiper and God. Islam has no hierarchical authority or priesthood. A learned Muslim chosen by each congregation leads the prayer.

The third Pillar is *Zakat*. One of the most important principles of Islam is that all things belong to God and that wealth is held in trust by human beings. *Zakat*—or charitable giving—"purifies" wealth by setting aside a portion for those in need. This payment is usually 2.5 percent of one's capital.

The fourth Pillar is **Fasting**. Every year in the Islamic lunar month of Ramadan, Muslims fast from first light until sunset. The fast is another method of self-purification.

The fifth Pillar is **Pilgrimage**. A pilgrimage to Mecca, or Hajj, is an obligation for those who are physically or financially able.

Muslims around the world celebrate Eid twice a year. Eid al-Fitr, also called Feast of Breaking the Fast, is an important religious holiday celebrated by Muslims worldwide that marks the end of Ramadan, the Islamic holy month of fasting.

Eid al-Adha, also called the Feast of Sacrifice, is the second religious holiday celebrated after Arafah. During Arafah, Muslims spend the day fasting. Eid al-Adha marks the remembrance of the prophet Abraham willing to sacrifice his son to God, but then God stopped him, and Abraham sacrificed a lamb or goat instead. Muslims are not allowed to eat pork because it is against the religion of Islam. Pigs are considered unclean. During the three days of Eid al-Adha, Muslims visit one another. Family and friends eat food together, and children receive presents.

HOLY TEXT

The Qur'an is considered the literal word of God, the Almighty (Allah in Arabic), revealed to Prophet Muhammad (peace be upon him) through the angel Gabriel. It was memorized by Muhammad and then dictated to his companions. The 114 chapters of the Qur'an have remained unchanged through the centuries. Literal translations of the Qur'an exist in almost all languages.

Muslims understand the Qur'an as God's final word. Islam means "surrender to God by serving God." It speaks of respecting all the previous scriptures and considers all "revealed" Abrahamic books as an article of faith in Islam.

Among the books mentioned in the Qur'an are the Torah (Taurat) revealed to Moses; the Book of Psalms (Zabuur), revealed to David; the Bible (Injeel) revealed to Jesus; and the Qur'an itself.

WOMEN AND MEN IN ISLAM

Under Islamic law, women have always had the right to own property, receive an education, and otherwise take part in community life. Men and women are to be respected equally. The Islamic rules for modest dress apply to both women and men. Men cannot expose certain parts of their bodies, wear gold or silk, and so on. If a particular society oppresses women, it does so in spite of Islam, not because of it.

MOGADISHU

I will never forget that day. The day that I left Sumaya, my cousin and best friend, still haunts me.

"Sumaya, what was your favorite part of Eid?" I ask, reflecting on how much fun we had yesterday as we celebrated Eid al-Fitr.

"I loved getting new clothes, and the food was amazing, but I would have to say that I liked dancing the best. How about you?"

Sumaya is grinning from ear to ear. Her smile always makes me happy. "Part of the fun for me was preparing for Eid, especially when my sister painted henna designs on my hands and arms. It seems that sometimes the anticipation is almost as fun as the celebration itself. Although dancing was probably the most fun thing for me, too."

As we walk home from school and I get closer to home, I see my *hooyo* watering the tulips and lilies that line the front of the house. She sure takes great pride in her beautiful flowers. "Hi, Zamzam. Dinner is almost ready. Come in and wash up."

"*Hooyo*, can I go to Sumaya's house after dinner? We want to go to the beach and go swimming."

"Zamzam, you can go after dinner once the dishes are done," says *Hooyo* expectantly.

"Thank you!" I run up to my *hooyo* and give her a big hug around her waist.

"Bye, Zamzam! See you after dinner!" Sumaya says cheerfully as she skips across the street to her house.

"Come on, Zamzam. You can set the table as I finish making dinner." As my hooyo heads into our house with a watering can in her hand, I quickly follow behind her. Soon dinner is ready, and I am eating cambuulo, a mixture of azuki beans, butter and sugar.

"*Hooyo*, I am done with the dishes, so I am heading over to Sumaya's house." I am out the door before I hear my *hooyo*'s response. Suddenly, I hear the rhythmic *thud, thud, thud* of the helicopters reverberating. My heart pounds. My throat clenches. The thuds grow closer. Louder. I know what that means. I will my legs to move faster. My *hooyo* runs out screaming. *Hooyo* shrieks, "Now! Run!" The sounds of the explosions fill my ears. Debris flies everywhere. I choke on the dust-filled air. I gasp for air. Shards of cement decimate the streets. We dart through the rubble. "Hurry! Keep going!"

As I turn back, I see that Sumaya's house is gone. And then there is stillness.

Did her family escape? Is she alive? That is what still haunts me.

NEW COUNTRY

Dear Sumaya,

I don't know if you will get this letter. I don't even have anywhere to send it to. But I don't have anyone to talk to. So I am writing because you are the only person I can talk to. I will pray that you know I am thinking of you and miss you.

It has now been a year since that fateful day. The day when the bombs fell on your house. The screams. The dust and debris flying everywhere. Sometimes I dream about it.

LANDING IN MINNESOTA

I look out the window of the airplane as it descends. At first, I see a bunch of tiny bright lights. As the airplane flies lower, I begin to notice the shapes of buildings and lots of roads. I have never seen so many tall buildings!

"Passengers, you have now landed in Minneapolis. It is 7:00 p.m. central time, and the temperature is forty-four degrees Fahrenheit. I hope you have enjoyed your flight," announces the airline pilot.

"*Hooyo*, I can't!" I abruptly stop right before the moving floor and my brother Hamze, who is right behind me, practically knocks me over.

"Zamzam, go ahead and step on to the moving walkway. Don't worry; you won't get hurt. The airport is large, and the motorized belt on the floor will help us get to the other side of the airport quickly so we can get our bags from baggage claim," insists my *hooyo*. Hamze obediently walks around me and follows *Hooyo*. If I don't want to get left behind, I have to step onto the moving walkway to keep up with everyone. Shakily, I put one foot in front of the other. I have to admit, after I get the hang of it, it is kind of fun to glide along.

My enthusiasm doesn't last very long, though. Soon, I see another level below. It is just too much. I plop down on the floor and whimper. *Hooyo* shakes her head in disbelief.

"What is wrong with you? These are stairs. You just need to make sure you hold the side rails as you walk down, one step at a time. Why are you so emotional today?"

Scared and nervous, I blurt out, "Everyone is so different here, and they have white skin. *Hooyo*, look! There is a lady with blonde hair wearing shorts. She is crazy!"

"Zamzam, shush. She is not crazy; she is just different," whispers *Hooyo*. "Now, if you want to see your aunt, uncle, and cousins, the only choice you have is to head down those stairs." Ifrah, my sister, Hamze, and my older brother, Abdi, trail close behind her.

It is a slow process, but I finally make it down the stairs. There weren't any stairs where I lived in Somalia, and I realize that I will be doing a lot of things for the first time.

There are people everywhere in the airport. I don't understand what anyone is saying, and they are staring at me. For the first time in my life, I feel very different. I have never been a minority. As I walk through the crowd toward the baggage claim, I notice that no one is wearing a hijab, and their skin is light. I tell myself that everything is just different, and that is okay. As I look around, I suddenly see people with brown skin like me. I recognize them!

"Ahmed! Mohamed! Oh wow! I didn't expect to see you guys here! Uncle Abdi!"

"Zamzam, we wanted to surprise you! Our family lives in Saint Cloud now. But when Uncle Hassan said you were coming to stay with his family in Minneapolis for a while, our dad said we could come down to visit for a couple of days!" exclaims Ahmed.

"Well, look at you! When was the last time you ate?" Uncle Abdi asks me as he scoops me up in his arms.

I admit to my uncle that I have been afraid to eat because the food looks and smells so different. Also, I don't know if any of the food contains pork. I have been drinking a lot of juice. "It has been a while."

"No sense standing around here. Let's head to my house for a good meal, and we can catch up there," insists Uncle Hassan. "I just have to warn you. When we get out of the airport, it is going to feel very cold outside. Except for a couple of months out of the year, Minnesota has a much colder climate than back home. Although it is March and spring is around the corner, it will continue to be cold for a while."

As soon as I step outside, I gasp as the cold air slaps me in the face. There is no way to prepare for the sting of the cold and the burning sensation in my lungs as I suck the air in. I shiver, trying to hold my hijab in place, while the wind whips it around.

Uncle Hassan tells us to walk a little quicker. "As soon as we get home, your aunt Zakia will have some warm stew waiting for you."

When we get to my aunt and uncle's house, the aroma of familiar food fills the room. All of a sudden, my stomach is growling. As my family sits down for a dinner of lamb stew and *sabaayad* (flatbread), it feels like everything is going to be okay.

Everyone is talking a hundred miles an hour and interrupting each other to get their stories out. My ears perk up when I hear Uncle Abdi talk. In between taking bites of stew, he tells my mom that we should move to Saint Cloud. It goes silent.

Uncle Abdi says, "The Saint Cloud community is welcoming, and you should move your family up there. The city has come a long way in accepting the Somali community in the past few years." Abdi looks at my *hooyo* intently as he licks his fingers after dipping *sabaayad* in and out of the stew.

He goes on to say, "At first, people wouldn't rent apartments to us. Our Somali families got jobs when they moved to Saint Cloud, but they had difficulty finding places to live. The apartment owners wanted to rent to people who not only had jobs but also had a credit history. Somalis weren't able to provide this information since they had recently immigrated. People in Saint Cloud didn't trust us because they didn't know if we were trustworthy. We looked and dressed differently." Abdi says that Somalis were also put in the same category as Africans who were born in the United States. "It was extremely challenging at first. When I first moved to Saint Cloud, there were twenty-five people living in a two-bedroom apartment. It took a city official to talk to the apartment owners. He told the apartment owners that they had to give the Somalis a place to live because they had jobs."

"If we move up to Saint Cloud, will we have a place to live?" my *hooyo* asks matter-of-factly. Despite spending many months in the refugee camp with us kids, not knowing when or where we would be going, *Hooyo* has never said or acted like she was scared.

"You can live with me and my family until you find a job. We will make sure you have what you need," replies Abdi, assuring my *hooyo*.

With conviction, *Hooyo* says, "If we can't make our home in Somalia, we will make our home in Saint Cloud. We will first spend a couple of months in Minneapolis visiting some of our family, and then we will move to Saint Cloud this summer."

Mohamed and Ahmed chime in excitedly, "Zamzam, once you move up to Saint Cloud, you can go to our school! It's really cool."

Ahmed adds, "There are lots and lots of books, and you should see the art room! I get to draw, paint, and work with clay. It is so much fun!"

"No, I will be in the eighth grade, like I was in Somalia," I insist.

Mohamed explains, "It is different here. They put you in a certain grade based on your age. That means that we will be in the same grade."

As my *hooyo* looks at Mohamed, she purses her lips and says, "We will see about that. My daughter is not going to be dropping down grades. She is a smart girl, and I expect her to move up, not down."

Dear Sumaya,

When we finally landed and walked into the airport, I was in shock. Everything is so different here. People seem to be in a hurry. There are even moving walkways so people can walk faster! You should see how people dress. Women wear short dresses, pants, and even shorts! Americans are very loud. Americans are big. EVERYTHING is big: roads, buildings, voices, and music. Just as I was trying to take it all in, I saw some of our family. Sumaya, I was so happy to see familiar faces!

Some of our aunts, uncles, and cousins are now living in Minnesota. I think you would like it here. You should hear the stories! I was told that there are malls for shopping with lots of colorful clothes. The girls get to dress how they want. Girls play sports just like the boys. You're not going to believe this, but there are even women leaders in this country!

Now, we need a miracle so you can come to Minnesota and live with me and our other cousins. I just can't stop thinking about you and your family, especially your three-year-old sisters. How can they possibly understand what is happening?

Oh, you know what else? Uncle Abdi, Mohamed, and Ahmed are living in Saint Cloud! When terrorists hit their home, they fled to a refugee camp in Kenya and then flew to America. Uncle Abdi told my hooyo that we should move up to Saint Cloud because there are opportunities to work and there is housing. I am hopeful that things will get better. Once my hooyo gets a job, we will be able to buy all the food and clothes that we want. I hear that Americans are rich. Now we can be rich, too! You will see for yourself someday. I know you will because I keep praying for a miracle.

THE FIRST DAY OF SCHOOL

Dear Sumaya,

I have so much to tell you. I don't even know where to begin. I am going to school at Abby Lake Elementary School in Saint Cloud, Minnesota. Believe it or not, I am in the sixth grade! It doesn't matter that I was in the eighth grade in Somalia. In the United States, you are in the same grade as other kids who are the same age as you. My mom is not happy about that. She told me that I am smart and that I should be in the eighth grade here, too. I have no idea if school will be easy or hard. Everything is so different. I sure wish you were here. Since we are the same age, you would be in the sixth grade with me! I have to admit, I am so nervous about my first day of school that my stomach is in knots, and I feel like I am going to throw up. So much for be-

ing brave! I know if you were here, everything would be okay. You always have a way of being carefree about things. Well, I am heading off to my first day of school. Wish me luck!

Mrs. Peterson, my sixth-grade teacher, has emerald-green eyes that light up her face when she smiles at us. Running her fingers through her short black hair, she introduces herself.

"Good morning, students. I would like to tell you a little bit about myself. I have two boys and a girl. My oldest son is off to college, but my other son and daughter are still in high school. Josh, my eighteen-year-old, talked me into skydiving with him last summer. Let me tell you, once is enough! Josh jumped out first, and as soon he jumped out, I asked myself, 'What was I thinking?' When you skydive, you basically jump out of an airplane wearing a parachute. Once you are in the sky, you pull your chute so the parachute opens up, and then you float to the ground."

Some of the students in my class seem to think that is cool. I wonder why anyone would jump out of an airplane on purpose. I am sure my teacher is a smart person, but that doesn't seem like a smart thing to do.

My teacher announces that she wants to get to know each of us better. Mrs. Peterson begins by sharing her racial autobiography. It is interesting to hear how her grandparents emigrated from Norway. Our first assignment is to write our own.

How much should I tell about myself? What will the other kids in my class think of me? I am going to need my *hooyo*'s help on this one. I know she will help me know what to say.

As I whip open the door to my apartment, I yell, "*Hooyo*, I'm home!"

"Zamzam! How was your first day of school?" *Hooyo* asks as she embraces me in a warm hug. As I sink into my *hooyo*, I look up at her, and she gives me her usual smile with big dimples that assures me that everything is going to be okay.

"My teacher's name is Mrs. Peterson, and she is really nice. We have a homework assignment where we have to write a racial autobiography. We have to tell about our culture and our families. I am afraid that the kids in my class will make fun of me if they know that I eat different foods from them, that I pray a lot, and that I don't celebrate Christmas. They might think I am weird. No one was mean to me, but some of the kids were staring at me in class today. *Hooyo*, the other kids in my class don't wear hijabs. I love my hijab, but I want to fit in. Now that I am living in Saint Cloud, am I supposed to dress like the other kids?"

"There is an African proverb that says, 'The daughter of a lion is also a lion.' In other words, no matter where you live, you will always be Somali. Be proud of who you are," insists my *hooyo*.

RACIAL AUTOBIOGRAPHY

Mrs. Peterson calls on me to go next. "Zamzam, please come up and share your story with us," my teacher coaxes, smiling and gesturing me to the front of the room.

I stand in front of the class and tell myself that I can do this. Trying to focus on what I am going to say, I take a big gulp, forcing the words out. "My brother Hamze is a year younger than I am. Although we are only a year apart in age, we don't really have that much in common personality-wise. Hamze can be easygoing and has a playful side, but he also is very quiet and reserved. I also have another brother, Abdi, who is a senior in high school, and a sister, Ifrah, who is in the tenth grade."

Mrs. Peterson thanks me for sharing my story and adds, "Does anyone have any questions for Zamzam?"

Emma, who sits in the front row, is listening intently to my story, cocks her head, and says, "I have two questions. First of all, what is Somalia like? I also want to know, why did your family come all the way here from Somalia?"

I am glad Emma asks these questions. I want everyone to know what Somalia is like; I mean, what it was like before the war.

"Somalia is a beautiful place. It has rivers and lakes and beaches that go on forever. We were very happy. My friends and I used to go wherever we wanted to play and go swimming. Although the war in Somalia began in 1991, it didn't affect my family until a year and a half ago. When our community in Mogadishu was attacked, we went to a refugee camp. Eventually, we left and came to the United States."

"How about food? What did you eat after you had to leave your home?" asks Emma, her eyes fixated on me.

"When we walked by the villages on the way to the refugee camp, people wanted to help my family. If the villagers had any food to spare, they would share it with us. Although there was very little food, we were lucky that we got any. There wasn't enough food for everyone, and a lot of people died from starvation."

I remember that horrible pain in my empty stomach that I tried to ignore but wouldn't go away.

"Although the civil war started in Somalia a long time ago, there continues to be fighting. My grandpa was the president of a tribe. He was very successful and well respected. The leader of another tribe was jealous of him, so his followers attacked my grandpa's tribe. Other tribes in Somalia began fighting, too, and this added to the civil war. There are also terrorists everywhere. Nobody feels safe. Terrorists try to recruit Somali people; and then they have to hide in the tall grass so the terrorists don't kill them for not wanting to fight."

Suddenly, I pause and look at the students in my class. Did I say too much? I didn't plan on saying so much, but I figured since Emma asked me, she wanted to know. As I look at all the white faces, I am wondering how much more I should tell. A couple of girls sitting in the back row are whispering and giggling. Are they making fun of me? I wonder who understands or even cares about my story. As I take a deep breath, I decide to continue sharing. "I have a lot of aunts, uncles, and cousins; like my family, many fled to the refugee camps in Kenya with hopes to come to the United States and start over. No matter where people fled, families were separated through death or destiny. That is how I ended up here."

As Emma bites her lip, she responds, "Wow! I had no idea. I couldn't imagine having to leave my home and my family."

I am relieved that I am done with my turn sharing.

Dear Sumaya,

I made it through my second day of school. I had to share my racial autobiography. When my name was called, my heart was pounding as fast as a drum roll, and my body felt like rubber. Weird that I have watched a bomb dropped on your house but this still makes me nervous. When I told my story, I left out details like how I didn't know if you were able to escape or if you were buried under the rubble (I still refuse to believe that); or how my family fled during the explosions, not being able to say good-bye to anyone and not knowing who survived. There are just certain things we don't talk about, like how we walked for weeks to get to a refugee camp. The scorching heat and the hot, dry wind that kicked up dust as we were walking. I remember being constantly thirsty. The bottoms feet hurt so badly because they were burned from walking on the hot sand. I didn't have a choice but to keep walking if I wanted to live. I did tell the class that, like many others, I left Somalia without my aabbe. Sumaya, you didn't even know this. How would you? When we were living in the refugee camp, my aabbe died from cholera when he drank the dirty water. Sometimes anger still bubbles up inside of me when I think about it. It is so unfair! My aabbe should be with me today, but he isn't because there wasn't a hospital in the refugee camp that we lived in. I am going to be a doctor so I can go back to Somalia and save other people from dying.

When I shared my racial autobiography, I told the class that I don't ever want to lose sight of my culture and that I am forever a Somali girl. My hooyo's words, reminding me that I will always be a Somali girl, are going through my mind as I say the last sentence. I want to believe it.

But things have changed. Some days I don't know who I am. Am I supposed to act like an American or a Somalian? I want to hang on to our culture, but there are things in America that I do like better. Like playing basketball during recess. I am not very good at basketball, but it is fun trying to throw the ball in the basket. My friends and I are planning to play soccer tomorrow. I am feeling frustrated and confused. I feel guilty for liking some things about my new country better; and other times I feel annoyed when people say stupid things like, "You're smart for a Somali girl."

Sumaya, you are the only person I can share this with because you understand me.

What I once knew for sure, I don't know anymore. My hooyo told me to be proud of our culture, but when I am told to go back to my country, and when I get made fun of for how I dress, that doesn't make me feel very proud of who I am.

SHARING FOOD

I try to fit in at my new school, but some days are overwhelming. There is so much to take in. It's really frustrating when I want to say something, but I don't know enough English to get the right words out. And it has been a long time since I have been in a formal school.

In the refugee camp, we made chairs by placing a piece of wood on rocks. The table where we sat was an old piece of wood. In some areas of Somalia, English was taught, but we learned in Somali. Now that I am in an American school, I realize there are rules like walking in a straight line down the hall with my class, not talking in class unless given permission to, and rules in the lunchroom.

Today's lunch includes chicken nuggets and fried rice . . . interesting. At least it isn't pork.

I have tried a lot of new foods since I have lived in Minnesota. Although most of it is nasty, I must say my favorite new food is pizza. I love cheese pizza!

Emma walks up to me and puts her hand on my shoulder. "Zamzam, come sit with me!"

"Sure! Sarah, you can sit with us, too." Sarah is new to Abby Lake Elementary also. She just moved to Saint Cloud from Worthington, a small town in southern Minnesota. Idil and Zakia, who moved here a couple of months ago from Somalia, join us.

Zakia looks at her plate, wrinkles up her nose, and says, "Ew, what is that? If it's pork, I am not eating it."

Emma picks up a chicken nugget and plops it in her mouth. "These are called chicken nuggets. I heard that they don't serve anything that has pork here so everyone can eat the school lunches. Try one. I think they are good."

Zakia bites slowly into a chicken nugget. "Hey, chicken nuggets are pretty good."

Idil takes a bite and spits it out in her napkin. "Those things are awful! Here, Zakia, you can have the rest of mine." She hands the rest of her chicken nuggets to Zakia.

I see Ms. Carol, the lunchroom monitor, out of the corner of my eye. She is heading to our table and has a stern look on her face as she stares at Idil.

"Girls, eat the food on your own trays. You aren't allowed to share food," scolds Ms. Carol as she put her hands on her hips, furrowing her eyebrows in a look of disapproval.

This really doesn't make sense to me. In the refugee camps, we were given barely enough food to survive. We always shared our food with each other to make sure no one would go hungry.

Emma has a puzzled look on her face. "What just happened?"

Feeling angry, I try to contain myself as I respond, "What just happened? We don't even have the freedom to eat what we want?"

"I know!" adds Idil. "Do you have any idea what it is like to be hungry, I mean really be hungry? I do. If I have food and someone else doesn't, I share, even if they aren't Somali. We take care of each other!"

Emma murmurs, "Wow. I wish more people would think like that. When I think of the saying, 'It takes a village,' it reminds me of your culture. In my culture, people tend to think more about themselves." She mumbles as she looks down, pushing the rice around with her fork.

EMMA'S VISIT

Dear Sumaya,

I have a new friend—Emma. On the outside, Emma looks very different from me. On the inside, we are very much alike.

Emma has long, curly red hair, hazel eyes, and freckles. She is very bubbly. Kind of like you. Emma and I seemed to have a connection immediately. You know how you just know when you are going to be friends with someone right off the bat? That's what happened between Emma and me. I wish you could meet her!

"Hey, Emma, do you want to hang out after school? I will ask my *hooyo* if you can stay for dinner. She is a really good cook," I say as Emma and I walk home together after school.

"Yeah, that would be fun. I will ask my mom if I can come over after I do my homework," says Emma enthusiastically, skipping along-side of me.

As we walk into our apartment building, I exclaim, "Okay, hopefully I will see you later!"

Emma waves back before she turns the corner and disappears into her apartment.

I am happy to see Emma when she shows up at my door. "Hi! I am glad your mom let you come over. Come on in. I want to show you something." I grab Emma's hand and walk her through my apartment, which doesn't have much furniture and has bare walls.

As we pass through the kitchen, I see my *hooyo* bent over the sink, washing our hijabs. "*Hooyo*, this is my friend Emma."

My *hooyo* picks her head up momentarily, smiling. "Nice to meet you, Emma." Then she leans back over the sink and goes back to washing our hijabs.

As we continue to walk toward the dining room, Emma asks, "Zamzam, why is your mom washing everything by hand? Don't you have a washing machine?"

"My *hooyo* is washing our hijabs, the beautiful scarves that you see me wear in school, by hand to keep them from wrinkling. When we lived in Somalia, there weren't any Laundromats. Clothes were washed in a big tub by hand. When we moved to America, my *hooyo* washed her hijab in the washing machine, but only once. The fabric came out wrinkled. That is why we still prefer to wash our hijabs by hand."

"Oh, that makes sense. What's that on your hand?" asks Emma as she points to my henna designs.

"Before you came over, my sister starting painting henna designs on my hand. That's what I want to show you. When she is done, I will have beautiful designs starting at my hands and going up my arms. Come on—I am excited for you to meet my sister, Ifrah. She can show you how she makes the henna designs. Ifrah is an amazing artist!"

Once Emma and I settle on one end of the long table, Ifrah smiles. "Hi! You must be Emma. Zamzam talks about you a lot. When I am done with Zamzam's henna tattoo, I can paint one on you. Don't worry, henna is a temporary dye, so it will eventually wear off," says Ifrah, holding a small brush in her hand and dipping it up and down into the inkpot.

"Sure, maybe a little one on my hand. I can't believe that you do that freehand! How do you paint such detailed patterns without your hand shaking or smearing the design?"

Laughing, Ifrah says, "I have had a lot of practice. We will be celebrating Eid al-Adha after Arafah, which starts tomorrow, so all the Somali women and girls will be getting henna tattoos in preparation for the celebration. We will be wearing henna designs again at the second Eid al-Fitr when we celebrate the end of Ramadan, and whenever someone gets married. Sometimes we wear the beautiful henna designs just because they are pretty."

"What is—" Emma starts to ask when my brother Abdi walks into the dining room with his friend Ayub.

"Oh, hang on! I have to get my hijab on quickly!" I shriek as I frantically put my hijab on. Ifrah ducks out of the room and minutes later shows up with her hijab on.

"Why did you have to put your hijab on?" asks Emma, wide-eyed with a look of confusion.

Adjusting my hijab to cover my hair, I explain, "Well, I don't always wear my hijab at home if there are only girls in the room. If there is a male in the room who isn't in my family, then I need to wear my hijab. If I go somewhere, I always wear my hijab."

Emma watches me adjust my hijab. "I wouldn't want to have my hair covered. I don't know if I would feel pretty. Plus, I wouldn't be able to jewelry. Why do you have to cover your hair?"

"Well, the first time my *hooyo* put a hijab over my head, I was in kindergarten. She explained it to me like this: 'Zamzam, you are like a precious pearl so beautiful inside a clamshell. You want others to know you for your beauty inside, and then they will know who you truly are. Your hijab is like a clamshell that protects your physical beauty. When you meet someone special, you will lift your hijab, and that special person will see your beauty inside and out.'"

Emma gives me a serious gaze, twirling her long, curly hair with her finger, "Interesting. I guess I never thought of it that way."

"I love wearing hijabs. I think my hair is plain black, and when I wear a hijab, I look more colorful . . . and I love fashion. Although most of the Somali girls at our school wear hijabs, they aren't required to wear them until they are fifteen years old. In Somalia, all the girls and women are covered from head to toe except for their faces and hands. Like I said before, it is a choice that women make. Most Muslim women choose to wear hijabs. I remember when our plane landed in Minneapolis and I walked into the airport, I thought the women were crazy! I had never seen a woman wear shorts before! My *hooyo* explained to me that in America it is okay for women show their hair, as well as their arms and legs. Talk about culture shock!"

Holding her hand steady as she is adding detail to Emma's henna tattoo, Ifrah comments, "Emma, what do you think of the design so far? Do you want me to paint henna on your other hand, too?"

"Yes, thank you! I love it so far. I hope it lasts a long time. Zamzam, you know how you were shocked the first time you saw what American women looked like? The first time that I saw a woman wear a long dress and her hair was covered by a long scarf, I thought it was weird."

"I know. When we see someone who looks so different from us, we think it is crazy or weird. If you take the time to get to know someone, you realize that person is not so different on the inside after all."

"Oh yeah, before your brother walked in with his friend, I was going to ask what Arafah means," says Emma.

Ifrah offers, "Arafah is when we fast and pray five times throughout the day. Then we celebrate Eid. There will be a feast, we will visit family, and kids get presents. It's sort of like when you celebrate Christmas." Ifrah points to me, and adds, "Zamzam especially likes getting new clothes."

"That is true! I love clothes and fashion!"

"That sounds like a lot of fun. How long do you fast for?" inquires Emma.

Ifrah chimes in, "During Arafah, we fast for one day, unlike Ramadan when we fast for a month."

Ifrah has finished painting Emma's henna design. "Hey, speaking of food, I wonder what *hooyo* made for dinner." As I start to get up from the table, Emma follows me to the kitchen.

"Emma, I hope you like your henna tattoo. Just be careful not to bump against anything so it can dry. Zamzam, you can help me set the table for dinner," instructs Ifrah as she stands up. "We need to set an extra plate for Ayub. I overheard Abdi asking *Hooyo* if his friend can stay for dinner."

I am anxious for Emma to try Somali food. I hope she likes it.

The fragrance of cumin and cardamom fill the kitchen, and I know what we are having for dinner. My *hooyo* leans over to set the plate of sambusas on the table; her long blue dress brushes against my chair. As she places the food on the table, I notice for the first time how weathered her hands look. It makes me think about what her hands have been through; how they continue to make me feel safe. I am proud of my *hooyo*.

Emma comments, "Mmm, something smells good. What are we eating for dinner?"

"Sambusas. They are turnovers filled with ground beef and spices," I reply.

After we say a prayer, it is time to eat. Emma looks a little confused and furrows her eyebrows, looking from the food to the plates and then to me. I think I know why.

"We eat our food with our hands. Go ahead and grab a sambusa and tell me what you think of it."

Emma reaches for a sambusa, puts it in her mouth, and smiles. "These are really good!" She reaches for another one.

"Emma, have you always lived in Saint Cloud?" asks Ifrah in between bites of sambusa and sips of tea.

"Yes, I was born here. My grandparents emigrated from Germany, and they live on a farm. Zamzam, you should go with me the next time I see my grandparents. My grandma makes homemade beef bratwurst and kuchen, a German coffee cake. We also eat a lot of fresh vegetables from the farm."

"Yeah, that would be fun. I would like to visit your grandparents' farm. Do they have animals?"

"Yep. There are lots of animals, including cows and chickens.

I have noticed that although we eat different foods, we also have some things in common. We both love fashion, and we both enjoy trying new things! I love my henna design. I can't wait to show my mom!"

Looking over at Emma as she admires her henna designs, I comment, "Yes, we do have some things in common! And you tried a new food today!"

Abdi pipes up, "*Hooyo*, we have our first soccer game tomorrow."

"That's great, Abdi! How is your team doing?"

"Our coach says that we are the best team that he has had in years," responds Abdi, sitting up a little straighter in his chair.

Emma adds enthusiastically, "I like to play soccer, too!"

"You? Play soccer?" Abdi smirks.

"Yep! And I am pretty good at it, too," Emma announces proudly. "Zamzam, we should play soccer at recess sometime!"

Thinking about how much fun it would be to try soccer, I respond, "That sounds like fun! I know Mohamed and Ahmed play soccer a lot. Maybe we could join them and get a game going!"

Abdi looks dumbfounded and doesn't reply.

"Well, I should probably get going." Emma stands up from the table, picking up her plate and turning to look at my *hooyo*, "Thank you for dinner. It was delicious! It was nice meeting you, Ifrah! Thanks for the henna designs. It was nice to meet you, too, Abdi."

After we clear our dishes, Emma and I walk to the door. "Thanks for inviting me over, Zamzam. I had a lot of fun! See you in school tomorrow!" exclaims Emma.

"Bye!" My life feels normal, if even for a moment.

STORY CLOTH

Dear Sumaya,

We had art class today. My teacher, Mr. Broden, read us a book about the pilgrimage of Hmong people across a war-torn country as the result of the Vietnam War. He told us how the story cloth was created to keep their experiences alive. After fleeing Laos, the Hmong were in refugee camps in Thailand. Women shared stories by embroidering pictures and events. Although they had embroidered pictures from the past, the story cloth was created for the benefit of sharing their stories with Americans. The story cloth links the past and the present.

I am realizing something important; not only does everyone have a story, but every story matters, no matter who you are.

When my teacher was talking about the story cloth and how threads are woven to tell them, it made me think that we are all connected with the thread of life. I don't have to try to be someone else to fit in where I am living.

I have been trying so hard to see where I fit in, trying to get others to accept me. I need to accept myself. I can now truly say that I am proud to be a Somali girl. I will forever be a Somali girl.

When Mr. Broden finishes reading the book, he tells us that our assignment is to create a story cloth about our own history and culture. Instead of embroidering on a cloth, we have a choice to use either markers or crayons and draw our cloth. I know what I want to include on mine.

We spend the next thirty minutes drawing. Mr. Broden mentions that he wants to allow the last ten minutes of class for volunteers to share their story. When the time comes, I raise my hand.

I think a lot about family and friends that were left behind, so I decide to share that piece of my life.

Pointing to the picture of palm trees amid houses lined up on my story cloth, I share, "My family lived in Mogadishu before the fighting began in Somalia. Kids helped by washing dishes, preparing food, pulling vegetables, and gathering firewood. And of course, we always found time to play. I had a lot of cousins and friends to play with, but my best friend was my cousin Sumaya, who's the same age as I am. We used to love swimming, playing jacks, singing, and dancing. That all changed when our houses were bombed. My family got out alive, but I don't know if Sumaya, who lived across the street from me, lived. I haven't seen her since that day."

Later, during recess, Emma comes over and sits on the swing next to me. "Zamzam, are you okay? Why didn't you tell me about this? I thought we were friends."

"We *are* friends. There are a lot of things that I haven't shared. Things that are hard to talk about. Today, I decided to share what I did because I want to honor my cousin Sumaya."

"Oh, I'm sorry. I didn't mean it like that. I just meant that you can talk to me about anything."

"No worries. You know when something bad happens to someone you love, and you can't do anything about it? And then you feel helpless? That's how I feel about my cousin. When bombs were dropped without warning, and everyone was running for their lives, I looked back and saw that Sumaya's house had been demolished. I don't even know if she made it out alive," I explain, looking up into the cloud-filled sky and trying to swallow back my tears.

"Zamzam, I am so sorry. I can't imagine what you have been through." Pausing, Emma adds, "I hope you find Sumaya some day."

I stop swinging for a moment and look over at Emma, "You just never know. Miracles do happen."

Emma looks at me with sad eyes and doesn't respond.

MINNESOTA WEATHER

I have been attending Abby Lake Elementary for about two months. The leaves on the trees have changed to beautiful shades of orange, yellow, and red, and they are starting to drop.

When I ask Mrs. Peterson why the leaves change colors, she explains, "When fall comes, the days get shorter and shorter. This is how the trees 'know' to get ready for winter. During winter, there isn't enough water or light for photosynthesis. The trees rest and live off the food they stored during the summer. The green chlorophyll also disappears from the leaves, which causes them to turn colors such as red, yellow, and orange."

It seems to make sense. I wonder what winter is going to be like. I have heard stories about how the temperature gets below zero. In Somalia, there isn't a cold season. The climate is tropical, and the temperature is usually around eighty degrees. I am both excited and nervous to find out what winter is like.

BUDGING IN LINE

Dear Sumaya,

At first, I thought everything was awesome here. It was all so new, and I thought my life would be better. I am starting to believe that people have a messed-up way of thinking.

We actually get in trouble for sharing food with each other. Today, Mohamed got into trouble for moving up in the line to get food in the lunchroom. I am so mad right now! Do you know that he got in trouble and he was sent to the very end of a very long line?

Then when he got upset, he was sent to the principal's office! I watched the whole thing happen.

I will never forget when I had to stand in a long line at the refugee camp to get food only to have no food left by the time I got into the front of the line. I had stomach pains from being so hungry, but there was nothing I could do about it. I had to wait to the next day to eat… but at least I got to eat. Mohamed and Ahmed told me a story about waking up one morning and their dad was gone. They were shaking their mom, trying to wake her up, but she never did wake up. Their world was turned upside down. Several days later, when their dad showed up at the camp, they found out that he journeyed out of the camp, desperately looking for a doctor for their mom. There was no doctor. Their dad, Abdi, explained to them that their mom had malaria from a mosquito bite. That is how she died.

Mohamed knows what it is like to suffer. Not only did he lose his mom, but he went from a life of living in comfort when his dad was a pharmacist and made good money to a life of struggle, often going days without food. At lunch today, Mohamed was going to make sure that he had food.

Just because we are now living in the United States doesn't mean that all of a sudden we have all the food that we want. You should have heard the stories that people have been sharing about the United States. If you work hard, you will be rich and have anything you want. Let me tell you that money does not grow on trees. We are still poor, and we still go hungry at times.

"Mohamed, go to the back of the line. Budging is not allowed," Ms. Carol, the lunchroom monitor, demands.

Mohamed starts kicking the wall and crying. "Mohamed, you need to go to Mrs. Williamson's office right now!" Ms. Carol makes up a tray for him to take to the principal's office so he doesn't miss lunch.

I can't believe what I am seeing. Joey sneers. "What's *his* problem? What a baby!" A couple of the boys at my table start laughing. My friends gasp.

"Stop it! Leave him alone. You have no idea what he has been through! Do you know what it is like to have to leave your home, have your mom die, and have barely enough food to survive?" I snap, fuming at the insensitive kids. I am on a roll. "You are *so* mean! I also think you are spoiled."

"Wow!" says Joey. "Sorry! It's not like he heard me."

Later that day, I catch up with Mohamed on the way home. "Hey, Mohamed, wait up! I saw what happened in the lunchroom today. What happened when you went to the principal's office? Did you get in trouble?"

"No." Mohamed walks slowly, hanging his head and kicking a rock down the sidewalk.

"Well, that's good! I was so mad when I saw what happened! What did you say to the principal?" I ask, feeling protective of Mohamed.

"It doesn't matter. I don't want to talk about it."

"Come on, Mohamed! It's me. I wouldn't have asked you if I didn't care," I encourage.

Mohamed slowly looks up and says, "I explained why I was trying to move to the front of the line to Mrs. Williamson. I told her that I missed breakfast because I was late for school, and then I was super hungry at lunch. I was trying to get through the line as fast as I could and cut in front of a student because I wanted to eat. I explained that the lunch lady told me to go to the back of the line. I was thinking about the lines I had to stand in for hours in the refugee camp to get food.

"She wanted to know more about what it was like in the refugee camp, so I explained that once we got to the refugee camps, we were called refugees. I also said that my dad got an identification card with the number of our family members on it. I told the principal that the United Nations provided food and tents for us to live in. We were given food like beans and rice. My dad also got a small allowance for buying vegetables. We were given just enough to survive," Mohamed shares as he looks off in the distance.

"After you explained it to her, what did she say?" I ask, encouraging Mohamed to continue, knowing that it is hard for him to open up.

"Mrs. Williamson said that she would talk to the lunch ladies. She also told me that I am not allowed to budge anymore. I told her that I won't. She did say one more thing," adds Mohamed.

"Mrs. Williamson explained that when you go through painful experiences and you survive, you develop something called resilience. She explained that resilience is the ability to recover from difficulties and to have strength. She told me that I have internal strength, and I am not supposed to let anyone make me feel less than or not good enough. Our principal said that I will accomplish whatever I make my mind up to do."

"You do have resilience. Anyone who survived the war and the refugee camps has resilience. Some people are coping better than others," I point out as I am thinking about the Somali people that I know that survived and how the war has affected them.

"Well, I am alive, and I made it to America, but this is not what I expected. Nobody gets me. I am tired of kids making fun of me. I am tired of not being able to say what I want because I don't always get the words right. I am tired of teachers feeling sorry for me. I can tell by the way they look at me. Also, my ears work. Sometimes teachers call us *those kids*. I want to go back home," Mohamed murmurs quietly, tears streaming down his face.

It makes me sad to see Mohamed have so much sadness and anger. I don't even know what to say to help him. How do I tell him that what he went through is real but not to feel sorry for himself? That he can be happy again? I wish I could tell him that everything is going to be okay. I wish that I could give Mohamed a hug and tell him that I care, but I know he would just pull back. In our culture, males don't show affection to females unless they are married. My stomach is in knots. I feel helpless. I can relate to him, also.

"I wish I could go back to Somalia, too. When we first got here, I was hoping that people would know what we went through and want to be nice. I wish someone would care enough to ask me about what I like to do or what things matter to me. I don't get it. Why do I feel bad inside because I look different on the outside? It seems like some people don't like me because my skin is brown and I dress differently from how they do. I had never heard of racism in Somalia. It makes me really sad and mad at the same time. All of us have feelings. People need to know that we are not a single story. I am not just a poor Somali girl who doesn't speak English very well. People don't realize that I wasn't even poor until I had to flee my home. And just because I don't understand everything my teachers say doesn't mean that I am not smart. And just because my skin is brown doesn't mean that I don't matter! If you think about it, it makes no sense that people think one color of skin is better than another. I think if people are going to judge, then they should judge people on their hearts . . . who they really are inside and how they treat people."

"Zamzam, you have really changed. I remember when you never expressed what was going on in your head. Now, you say what is on your mind, and you talk about your feelings," notes Mohamed, looking me square in the eyes.

"I know. I guess I am tired of being treated like I am less than a person because I look different from other people.

I have learned so much in this past year, trying to figure out where I fit in. I don't want to feel that way anymore. I don't want anyone else to feel that way, either."

WINTER WEATHER

Dear Sumaya,

It is now January, and I can officially say that I know what extreme cold feels like. You can't imagine it. When you breathe in, you feel the freezing air in your lungs. If you breathe through your nose, you can even feel your nose hairs stick together, and your eyelashes can get layers of frost on them!

Of course, we now have coats, boots, hats, and gloves. It helps a little bit. When it's really cold, I go outside only when I have to, which means walking to and from school.

If it weren't cold like this, I wouldn't mind the snow so much. It is white, cold, and wet, and it sticks together when you pack it into a ball. Hamze and I had a snowball fight last weekend. I wasn't sure what to expect, but it didn't even hurt to get hit by the snow. It was a blast!

MORE CHALLENGES

In the sixth grade, we rotate classes for reading and math. Ms. Emmett is my reading teacher. I dread going to this class because Ms. Emmett doesn't like me. I mean she *really* doesn't like me.

After she graded our reports yesterday, Ms. Emmett told us that our parents needed to sign the bottom of our papers to show that they read them and saw our grades.

"Students, take out your papers and put them in the basket; then turn to page 32 in your books," instructs Ms. Emmett, pointing to the basket on her desk.

I pull my paper out, and the girl next to me snatches it out of my hand. She shows it to her friend, and they giggle.

"Give it back!"

They point to my mom's signature and taunt, "What is *that* supposed to say?"

"It's my mom's name." She wrote it in Arabic, so the letters are slanted, and I think it probably doesn't look like American letters.

"Give me my paper back!" I cry as the girls pass the paper around the room.

I try to get the attention of my teacher. "Ms. Emmett, they won't give me my paper back."

"Sit down!" snaps Ms. Emmett, glaring at me.

I sit down, look at the girls, and say, "You're stupid!"

"Ms. Emmett, Zamzam called us *stupid Americans!*"

I can't believe this is happening. Why are they lying? Why won't anyone listen to me?

"Zamzam, don't you ever call anyone a *stupid American* again!" snaps Ms. Emmett, staring down at me with her hands on her hips.

"Ms. Emmett, I didn't. I said *they* were stupid because they were making fun of my mom's writing and they wouldn't give me my paper back. That's what I was trying to tell you when you made me sit back down. You weren't listening to me." I am so frustrated!

"Go to the office *right now*! You will learn that you don't call anyone a *stupid American*."

After school, *Hooyo* asks me how my day was, and I tell her what happened.

As she furrows her eyebrows, *Hooyo* immediately picks up her cell phone and calls Ms. Emmett.

I sit at the kitchen table and hear everything.

I don't think my *hooyo* allowed Ms. Emmett to get a word in edgewise. "I understand that my daughter was bullied in school today. It is bad enough when students bully each other, but you are an adult, and you should know better! How dare you accuse my daughter of saying something that didn't come out of her mouth! I will not tolerate you treating my daughter like she has less value than an American. If you would have actually listened to her and respected her as a person who matters, then you wouldn't have accused her of saying something she didn't and being someone that she isn't! My request to you is that you listen before you jump to conclusions. I expect you will hear what my daughter has to say next time so something like this doesn't happen again," scolds my *hooyo,* whipping her hijab off her head and throwing it on the floor as she paces back and forth.

Dear Sumaya,

Today in class, I was bullied for being a Somali girl. A couple of girls in my class put words in my mouth, and my teacher wouldn't even listen to me! Some of the kids in my class make fun of anyone who is different from they are. But are we really that different?

If we take the time to get to know each other before jumping to judgment, this world would be a better place. People would have more friends because they would realize how cool it is to learn about someone who has had different life experiences but has the same desires.

It shouldn't matter where you were born or what color your skin is; everyone wants to belong, to be accepted. Everyone wants to be valued. Everyone wants to be loved. Some people spend their whole lives not knowing what it feels like to be loved. One thing I can say for sure is that although we don't have expensive cars or the latest electronic gadgets, I know I am loved.

Sumaya, I wish with all my heart that I could go back in time when things were simple. We really did lead a peaceful life in Somalia. . . before our houses were bombed. I pray that you are alive. . . and know that you are loved!

SOAP INCIDENT

"Students, if you need to use the bathroom, this is a good time. Otherwise, wait quietly in line." As Emma and I stand at the sink washing our hands, we notice that there isn't any soap in the dispenser. Emma tells Mrs. Peterson that we are out of soap.

"Idil, please head back to the classroom and bring some soap. There isn't any left in the dispenser by the sink."

Idil smiles widely as she skips down the hallway toward our classroom. Before long, I see her beaming; she is carrying an entire soap *dispenser* back to our teacher.

"Here is the soap, Mrs. Peterson," Idil proudly announces. "It took me a few minutes to find the soap in our classroom, but then I found it by the sink. It wasn't easy, but with a few hard yanks, I was able to pull it off of the wall."

Mrs. Peterson keeps a straight face, but it looks like she is about to laugh. "Thank you for bringing the soap, Idil." I am glad that no one made fun of Idil or tried to embarrass her. I bet Mrs. Peterson will be a little more specific next time!

BIASES

We just learned how to write a biography in class and Mrs. Peterson used Abraham Lincoln as a subject. She taught us how to find key words, put the important words into sentences, and organize the information.

I learned about Abraham Lincoln's birth and early years, education, accomplishments, and then his later years and death. Mr. Lincoln helped people during the Civil War in the United States. He fought to end slavery and won. I am living in Minnesota because of the civil war in Somalia. I want someone like Abraham Lincoln to stop the fighting in Somalia.

Mrs. Peterson says, "Now that we have been through the process of creating a biography, I have assigned you to groups of four to create a biography on a historical person. Please go through the list of historical figures on the sheet that has been passed out, and let me know who your group has chosen to write about."

I feel sick to my stomach when I find out who is in my group. I like Sarah and Abdi, but Joey is mean. He thinks he is all that and makes fun of everyone. He even mimics our teacher when she isn't looking.

I don't know any of the names on the list, so I tell my group that I don't care whom we write about. When Sarah walks over to Mrs. Peterson's desk to announce that we have chosen Paul Revere, Joey looks me square in the eye and says, "Wow. You don't even know who Paul Revere is? If you are going to live in America, you had better learn about who is important. You should go back to the country of Africa."

I know what I want to say, but I am not going to. He made fun of me last week, too. Maybe if I ignore him again, he will leave me alone.

Well, that tactic doesn't work. Joey just won't stop!

"Oh, and by the way, you even dress funny. You are just a poor Somali girl who doesn't know anything."

That's it! Trying to hold back the tears, I blurt, "You don't even know me. You don't take the time to get to know me because you don't even care. If you did, you wouldn't have said what you just did!" I know I should stop, but I don't. "I was born black just like you were born white! I didn't *choose* to have a war in Somalia. Everything in my life has been stripped from me! Imagine living in a community where everyone cares about each other, is respectful, and is generous. Family and friends spend time together, living in peace. That is what I lost. Imagine a beautiful country with palm trees, sandy beaches, and the ocean rolling in and out with the waves. That's Somalia. That is where I used to live and play. Imagine having all the fresh food that you want!"

Hot tears stream down my face. My body trembles uncontrollably.

"*That* is what I lost. Now I see food processed and stored in boxes and the freezer. I didn't choose to leave my country. My family was *forced* out! So do you think I *want* to live here? No! But I do because I don't have a choice!"

For a moment, I look up, and I see that my teacher is helping another group. She doesn't even see what is going on!

"I just want to be treated like a person! And for your information, I have just as much value as you. So either be nice or stop talking to me."

My heart is pounding so hard that I can feel it thumping in my chest.

"Oh, and by the way, Africa isn't a country. *It's a continent!*"

I can't wait to go home. I just want my *hooyo*. I wish the stupid war didn't happen so I could go back to Somalia. I am tired of people trying to make me feel bad for being me!

I am a good person, and I am trying to fit in to this new way of living and fit into the new culture while still being me.

I run all the way home and fling open the door, "*Hooyo! Hooyo!*" I am no longer trying to hold back the tears and they come flooding out.

"What is wrong? Slow down so I can understand you," *Hooyo* says in a soothing voice. "Come over here and sit down," continues *Hooyo*, pointing to spot next to her on the sofa.

"I am so confused. Most days I like school, and I love my teacher, but lately I don't what to do. It's like I am not good enough because I was born this way."

"Zamzam, what are you talking about?" *Hooyo* asks, trying to understand me.

"I am trying to be good, but when someone tells me to go back where I came from, I wonder who else is thinking the same thing. I want to go back to Somalia! I am proud of my culture and who I am, but I don't understand why people are always judging me. My teachers act like they feel sorry for me sometimes, and I am starting to wonder if I even belong here."

"What happened in school today? Obviously, something upsetting happened for you to say that and to be so sad."

At this point, I tell my *hooyo* the whole story about what happened and what Joey said to me.

Leaning over, *Hooyo* pulls me closer to her and gives me a hug. She assures me that she is going to talk to Mrs. Peterson, insisting that my teacher should know what happened. She goes straight to the phone and calls Mrs. Peterson.

"This is Zamzam's mom, Nimo. I would like to talk to you about an incident that happened in school today. Is this a good time for you to talk?"

"Yes, definitely. What incident are you talking about?"

"When Zamzam came home after school today, she was quite upset. And I must say that I don't blame her. A boy in her class was bullying her, commenting on how she dresses, and he told her that she should go back to her own country. I understand that sometimes kids say things that they hear from adults, but that still doesn't make it okay for him to talk like that to my daughter.

"You know that we came to the United States as refugees. We were scared, didn't speak English, struggled to find jobs, and knew that a lot of white people didn't even want us here. The Somali community lives in apartments, and there isn't anywhere for our children to go out and play like they could back home before the war. It is also difficult to get used to the food here. Winters here are also bitter, and the weather in Somalia is much warmer. So you see, we continue to experience struggles here. What I find interesting is that one culture would think it is superior over another. We are trying to assimilate into our new environment, but we are proud of our culture and values. Please try to understand that. I am sharing this in hopes that you will educate others and be aware of biases in your classroom and school.

Zamzam has had plenty of struggles. She really is a smart girl. Please just treat her as a person who has potential, and challenge her. I guarantee you that she will exceed your expectations."

"I care about Zamzam, and I know she is a very bright girl. I will be sure to reflect it in my teaching, and I will challenge Zamzam to reach her potential."

FLASHBACK

Dear Sumaya,

While we were outside playing today at recess, a helicopter flew by. The rumbling was deafening. My heart started pounding, but I kept reminding myself that I was safe. I had the most horrible feeling. It brought me back to that day. I could hear screams in my head, see people running for their lives, the haze of the dust-filled air... debris flying.

I saw Hassan sprint into the nearby cornfields as fast as a cheetah chasing its prey and then hide. The recess monitors obviously didn't understand why he ran into the cornfields because they just got mad when he went beyond the boundaries allowed during recess. I think they panicked a little because Hassan took off. They couldn't find him. I heard one

of the recess monitors calling the assistant principal on her walkie-talkie, requesting help to find Hassan. After about fifteen minutes, they finally found him. The recess monitor confronted Hassan and told him that he was not allowed to leave the playground area during recess.

Hassan burst out crying. Hassan just moved here from the refugee camp in Kenya. He doesn't understand English very well; he couldn't explain why he ran into the cornfields and didn't understand what the recess monitor was saying.

I knew that his adrenaline just kicked in, and he was in survival mode—just like I felt. Since I saw the whole thing happen and I didn't want Hassan to get into trouble, I explained to the recess monitor and the assistant principal that Hassan was probably having a flashback (big word, I know—Abdi taught me that one).

I told them Hassan flashed back in his head to a time when bombs were being dropped. He just got scared and ran. I thought the recess monitor finally understood what was going on because she comforted Hassan and told him he would be safe here. She hugged him and warned him that helicopters or airplanes fly overhead, but he is safe.

RACIAL TENSION

Dear Sumaya,

You're not going to believe this, but there are Somali kids who were born in America that don't want anything to do with Somalis who are new to this country. When I was hanging out at Emma's house yesterday, Mohamed, her neighbor, came over to play with her brother. Apparently, he likes to be called Moha. When I told him that I thought it was kind of weird that he didn't call himself Mohamed, he just gave me a dirty look and walked away.

Emma said she thinks he uses slang because he doesn't want to be seen as a Somali. She shared with me that Moha was born in the United States, and he has told her brother that he considers himself to be an American.

He said that he relates to the white culture more than the Somali culture because of how he was raised and because he speaks English.

Emma told me that when Moha talks with Somali kids who are new to the country, he thinks that he is better than they are. Hamze found this out firsthand. He came home from school today, sobbing uncontrollably. When Hooyo was finally able to console him, Hamze told her what had happened.

Students were told that they would be partnered up to complete a science experiment. When Hamze asked Moha to be his partner, Moha looked at him in disgust and said that he wasn't going to be seen with him, adding that he was nothing like Hamze and that he was an American.

Moha called him a know-it-all that didn't even speak English very well!

Sumaya, just because my brother is smart and works hard in school, kids pick on him. Especially Moha. Seriously? It makes me angry that people can be so cruel.

Hooyo told Hamze and me that she has noticed some Somali people who were born in the United States don't relate to Somalis like us. It's like they look down on us. But Hooyo held Hamze in her arms and told him to keep his chin up and keep on being a good boy.

EQUAL OPPORTUNITY

It is May, and the weather is finally warmer. I'm looking forward to recess. I've been sitting in the computer lab all morning taking the state-mandated reading assessment. I need to get rid of some of my energy. I usually either shoot hoops with my friends or just hang out.

Today, we decided to join the boys for a game of soccer. Some of the boys get very competitive, and I am okay with that; but sometimes the games get out of hand, and fights break out.

"Hey, Abdi, can we play soccer with you guys?" I ask politely.

Abdi snaps, "No, you can't play. Go away!"

"Who put *you* in charge?" I am now madder than a wet cat. I tell the recess monitor about it and ask if my friends and I can talk to the principal. She agrees.

Idil, Zakia, and I march down to Mrs. Williamson's office, and we ask her if we can talk to her.

Mrs. Williamson tucks a piece of her blonde hair behind her ear and straightens her dress as she stands up. "Of course, girls. Please come on in."

Idil blurts, "We asked the boys if we could play soccer, and they told us we couldn't and to go away."

"You have a right to play soccer just as much as the boys do. I will have a chat with them about including you. How about if you start your own game of soccer?" suggests the principal.

I speak up. "We can't because there is only one soccer ball. The boys act like they own it and they are in charge."

"Well, we can solve that problem! I will buy another soccer ball, and you can play soccer. I think it's wonderful that you like to play soccer. Sports are a great way to get exercise, learn a new skill, and have fun with your friends. Let me know if you ever want me to show you some basketball moves," declares Principal Williamson.

"Thank you!" all three of us chime in at once.

"You are very welcome!" replies Mrs. Williamson.

As we skip down the hallway on our way back to class, Idil declares, "Girl power!" My friends and I put our hands in the air and give each other a high five.

Dear Sumaya,

Something interesting happened today. Since girls get to play sports in America, my friends and I decided that we would play soccer for recess. The boys were so mean! They wouldn't let us play and told us to go away, so we went to the principal's office to tell Mrs. Williamson. She wasn't happy. Mrs. Williamson told us that no matter who you are, you have the same rights and opportunities. It felt really good to hear her say that; and you know what? I believe her! I do have the same rights as anyone else to follow my dreams. I am going to work hard and follow my heart to accomplish whatever I want to!

SUMAYA

It was quite a day. I am exhausted. As I climb into bed and pull the covers up, my mind drifts to what life was like before my world was turned upside down.

"Sumaya, look!" I exclaim, pointing to our family and friends dancing on the beach as musicians tap on their drums and sing happy songs. Eid is finally here, and I am so excited for this day of celebration. We giggle at the sight of our parents dancing to the music.

Sumaya grabs my hand. "Come on, Zamzam! Let's go dance!"

Everything about this day is perfect. There is a soft breeze swaying the palm trees back and forth. Ocean waves roll in, licking the sandy shore. My hooyo *has spent the last couple of days helping to prepare a feast for this special day as we celebrate the end of Ramadan.*

"Zamzam, I am getting hungry. Let's get something to eat."

"Wow! Look at all that food . . ."

"Zamzam, it is time to get up and get ready for school," announces *Hooyo* as she flips my bedroom light on.

I just want to stay in bed and finish my dream. A dream that seemed so real. Some days I want to turn back time.

Mrs. Peterson announces to our class that we have a new student. She reminds us to make our new classmate feel welcome, adding that her name is Sumaya. I notice that the new student is wearing a purple hijab and a matching dress. When she turns to face me, our eyes lock. I don't believe it! My prayers have been answered!

I cry out, *"Allahu Akbar! Allahu Akbar!* Sumaya, you are alive!" I run to Sumaya, and we hug each other tightly. I don't want to let her go.

Mrs. Peterson quickly walks over to Sumaya and me. "Girls, I don't understand Somali, so I don't know what you are saying. Zamzam, why don't you take Sumaya out in the hall and come back into the classroom in a few minutes when you are ready? I would like to talk to both of you when our class goes to recess."

We quickly move into the hallway. Through her tears, Sumaya looks at me with big eyes and pleads, "Why did you leave me? Why did you let my sisters die? My *aabbe* and my brother were killed when our house was bombed. At first, right after our home was demolished, I hid in the open spaces under the debris with my *hooyo* and sisters. I knew that when the terrorists showed up, they would go into the nearby building that was still standing. Once night fell and it was dark outside, we managed to escape.

"Oh, Sumaya. I am so sorry," I say gently as I wipe the tears off her face.

"We had to walk for many, many miles, trying to reach a refugee camp, sometimes going days without food. My sisters died because they weren't able to keep up, and there wasn't enough food for everyone. My life has been a nightmare."

My heart floods with emotion. I swallow the lump in my throat, trying not to cry. As I grab both of Sumaya's hands and look into her tear-filled eyes, I say, "Sumaya, I didn't leave you. I didn't leave you! I clearly remember the day the bombs exploded, leaving your house demolished and rubble strewn everywhere. When my family fled and I didn't see you, I wanted to believe you were alive. There hasn't been a day that has gone by when I haven't thought about you and your family!"

"Oh, Zamzam. I can't believe we are together again! I have missed you so much. I thought you had forgotten about me."

"I can prove to you that I never forgot about you, Sumaya! I wrote you letters, hoping and praying every day for a miracle, not knowing if you would ever see them. And now you are here. My dear Sumaya! You are safe! Know that you are now safe!" I embrace Sumaya again, her body no longer trembling, and we both sob tears of joy.

LAST DAY OF SCHOOL

The year seems to fly by. It is the last day of school, and we are filing into the gym, one class at a time. The school assembly celebrates our hard work and accomplishments. I have become a good reader. I paid attention in class. I read every night. It has been hard work. But when the principal calls my name to announce I'm one of the top readers of the class, I know it was worth it! I am so proud! I know that I am on the right track to realize my dreams. I know that I will have opportunities that my family back home could only dream of. I know in my heart that I am going to become a doctor someday and then go back to Somalia to heal others.

Through my eyes, I see a society that takes the time to get to know me before it judges me, a society that is not only tolerant but appreciates my uniqueness. I believe love is the most important thing in the world. When you know better, you do better, right?

Through my eyes, I see myself as a person who is strong and has the determination to make this world a better place.

GLOSSARY

Aabbe—father

Bias—prejudice in favor of or against one thing, person, or group compared with another, usually in a way considered to be unfair

Civil war—a war between political factions or regions within the same country

Clan—a group of close-knit and interrelated families

Eid al-Adha—meaning "Festival of Sacrifice"; the second of two religious holidays celebrated by Muslims worldwide

Eid al-Fitr-an important religious holiday celebrated by Muslims worldwide that marks the end of Ramadan

Emigrant—a person who leaves his or her country in order to permanently settle in another

Five Pillars—five basic acts in Islam, considered mandatory by believers; they make up Muslim life, prayer, concern for the needy, self-purification, and the pilgrimage

Hijab—a traditional scarf worn by Muslim women to cover their hair and necks and sometimes their faces

Hijri calendar (Islamic calendar)—lunar calendar consisting of 12 months in a year of 354 days

Hooyo—mother

Immigrant—a person who migrates to another country, usually for permanent residence

Kuchen—a yeast-raised German coffee cake, often containing fruit

Mogadishu—the seaport capital of Somalia

Prejudice—opinion that is not based on reason or actual experience

Ramadan—the daily fast that is rigidly enjoined from dawn until sunset during the ninth month of the Muslim calendar

Refugee—a person who flees for refuge or safety, especially to a foreign country, as in time of political upheaval, war, and the like

Refugee camp—a temporary settlement built to receive refugees

Somalia—a country that occupies the tip of a region commonly referred to as the Horn of Africa, east of Ethiopia

Somali civil war—an ongoing civil war taking place in Somalia

Stereotype—a thought that can be adopted about specific types of individuals or certain ways of doing things; these thoughts or beliefs may or may not accurately reflect reality

DISCUSSION QUESTIONS

Define prejudice and bias. While they are not the exact same thing, they are related. What examples of prejudice do you see in the book? Of bias? How do either affect Zamzam?

Compare how Zamzam's life in Somalia is like yours.

Evaluate the role food plays in family life.

Make a chart like the one below. List foods mentioned by culture in the story. What do you notice about the types of food? What about when it is being eaten?

Somali	American	German

What role does food play in your family?

Why does *Hooyo* react the way she does when things happen to Zamzam? Did her reactions surprise you? Why or why not?

Recall what you have seen Zamzam's *hooyo*'s hands doing. Why would they be weathered? What else do you think she might be doing that would cause that to happen either now or in the past?

Analyze what the author means when she says Zamzam's family does not talk about certain things.

Determine why it is hard to Zamzam to hold tight to the quote, "The daughter of a lion is also a lion." Why is she so conflicted?

Choose any character in the story. What is the importance of resilience in his or her life? How can resilience help?

A lot of culture clashes come from not understanding nuances in language. What did Mrs. Peterson really want Idil to do when she asked her to get the soap? Extension: while this is not an idiom, idioms cause problems for people learning new languages. Look at idioms from other cultures. Would you be able to understand what they mean?

Why did Moha, a second-generation Somali student look down on first-generation students?

Compare and contrast the Somali and Hmong refugees.

Infer what Zamzam wants you to know when she says, "We are all connected with the thread of life."

What is the significance of the title of the book? Determine what you believe the author wants you to walk away knowing.

EXTENSION PROJECTS

Research the history of Somalia. Make a map of Somalia with pictures included.

Research henna, design and its history. What has it meant in the past for women to wear henna? What does it mean now? Where else in the world do women/girls wear henna?

Compare and contrast the Somali American immigrants' food and dress to that of at least two cultures that immigrated to the United States in the past, such as Italian and Irish. How were the cultures from the past received? Do you see a pattern? What eventually happened? Extend by predicting what you think will happen with Somali immigrants and refugees eventually if the pattern holds.

ABOUT THE AUTHOR

Tammy Wilson is an elementary principal in Saint Cloud, MN. Working in a school with a high Somali population, she saw a need for her students to see themselves represented in literature. This compelled her to write a book to not only inspire children, but also educate adults. Tammy has three adult children who live in Minnesota.

She has a taste for adventure, spending time in nature, listening to live music, and traveling to new destinations.